DIRTY JOE THE PIRATE

A True Story

WORDS BY **BILL HARLEY** • PICTURES BY **JACK E. DAVIS**

HarperCollinsPublishers

Library of Congress Cataloging-in-Publication Data is available.
ISBN 978-0-06-623780-0 (trade bdg.) – ISBN 978-0-06-623781-7 (lib. bdg.)
Typography by Jeanne L. Hogle
1 2 3 4 5 6 7 8 9 10
❖
First Edition

01 09

To my old pal Richard Walton and all
the other pirates in Pawtuxet Cove

—B.H.

For little Hugo, who often searches for pirates
while walking with Grandma Jay after preschool

—J.E.D.

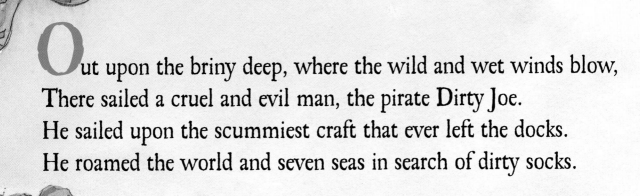

Out upon the briny deep, where the wild and wet winds blow,
There sailed a cruel and evil man, the pirate Dirty Joe.
He sailed upon the scummiest craft that ever left the docks.
He roamed the world and seven seas in search of dirty socks.

His one good eye surveyed the seas, searching for some ship,
And when he spied a boat out there, he'd sneer and lick his lips.
"All hands on deck," he'd order. "There's treasure to be had!"
He'd shake his one fist in the air and laugh like he were mad.

He'd fire a cannon 'cross their bow and board the other craft,
Then make the crew take off their shoes, and with a horrid laugh,
He'd tie the sailors all up tight and rob them of their socks,
Then leave their ship a-floundering to run up on the rocks.

The socks he took from other ships, you'll be surprised to learn,
He tied upon his rigging lines that stretched from bow to stern.
They flapped and fluttered in the breeze, five hundred little flags—
And the smell that those old socks gave off was enough to make you gag.

Till one day, as he sailed his ship somewhere near Mandalay,
His lookout spied another boat beating 'cross the bay.
"Ah ha!" said Joe. "Let's get that boat. We'll catch her now, by thunder.
For sure as I am Dirty Joe, there's socks there we can plunder."

The pirates cheered and set the sails to catch up with their prey.
They sharpened up their knives and swords, their boat danced in the spray.
But suddenly the cheering stopped. The wind, it gave a moan,
For on the other ship there flew a flag of skull and bones.

From mast to mast, from bow to stern, flying everywhere
There flapped and snapped five hundred pairs of pilfered underwear—
Boxers big and boxers small, with stripes and polka dots,
And tighty-whities hung there too, like the ones your grandpa's got.

Lined up on that other deck, armed with swords and knives,
Was a sight that made the men all shake and fear for their own lives.
One hundred pirate women waved their daggers and their swords,
And a woman pirate captain yelled, "Girls, let's climb aboard!"

"It's Stinky Annie," someone said, "and her band of smelly varmints.
She captures every boat she can and takes their undergarments."
"Then all is lost," another said. "We haven't got a chance.
You can't be a pirate if you don't have underpants."

"You lily-livered lunks of lard," lashed out Dirty Joe.
"What sort of pirates are you lads? That's what I want to know.
We'll show them, we'll take their ship, we'll tie them up!" he roared.
"We'll take their socks and sneakers, too, and throw them overboard!"

The pirates there with Dirty Joe screamed and cheered and yelled.
Someone blew a whistle, someone rang the bell.

As the boats drew near, the pirates cursed and muttered,
While a thousand pairs of underwear and socks all flapped and fluttered.

And as their ships came closer still, Joe's men all could see
That Stinky Annie was as scary-looking as could be.
Her mouth was twisted in a sneer, one arm was but a hook,
And with her one good evil eye she gave a withering look.

Finally the two ships met. On the waves they rocked.
"Get them now, boys," Joe cried out. "Take off all their socks!"
But even as the men attacked the women waiting there,
Stinky Ann called to her crew, "Girls—get their underwear!"

It was an awful battle, a loud and raucous fray—
At first it seemed that Dirty Joe would win and have his way,
Until Joe's first mate noticed that Stinky Annie's crew
All were fighting barefoot—they had no socks or shoes.

Stinky Annie lowered her sword. They peered at one another.
"Wait," she said, "I see it now—you're Joe, my little brother."
"That's right," said Joe. "You're sister Ann, you bounced me on your knee.
Put down your sword, give up this fight. Please don't do this to me!"

Stinky Annie gave a smile, a tear came to her eye.
All her crew looked on in awe. They'd never seen her cry.
"Little Joey, how are you?" she asked. "How have you been?"
"I'm just fine, dear sister Ann," he said, and gave a grin.

Stinky Annie came aboard and cornered Dirty Joe.
She said, "I want your boxers now, in case you didn't know."
Then Dirty Joe looked up and said, "Before you have your fun,
Your face looks quite familiar, you remind me of someone."

"What's the point?" a man called out. "Why make all this fuss?
If we can't get their dirty socks, what's in it for us?"
"No!" screamed Joe. "Don't give up now!" But he spoke the words too late,
And Stinky Annie and her crew quickly sealed their fate.

"Good," said Annie, "that's great news." Her one eye shone and danced.
"Now do just what I say, you squirt. I want your underpants."
"But Annie, you're my sister," Joe blubbered and he whined.
"Stow it, Joey," Annie said. "I haven't got the time."

"Just 'cause I'm your sister, it doesn't mean I care.
I'm a pirate—that's me job—I want your underwear."
So Dirty Joe surrendered and did what his sister said.
And when he did, it's safe to say, more than his face was red.

Stinky Annie sailed away, and still she roams the seas,
With her brother's boxers high above, flapping in the breeze.

And Dirty Joe, he sailed home, close to the Bay of Fundy.
He's not a pirate anymore, because he has no undies.

That's the finish of this tale. It's silly and it's done.
But there's a lesson here that I'd impart to everyone:
If you've got an older sister, then I feel bad for you,
'Cause just as long as she's alive, she'll tell you what to do.